A Unique Start From 6 Feet Apart

A Book About Returning to the Classroom During a Pandemic

Written by: Emily Oquendo   Illustrated by: Hina Mahmood

A Unique Start From 6 Feet Apart

A Book About Returning to the Classroom During a Pandemic

E. Oquendo
Copyright © 2020 Emily Oquendo

Independently Published

ISBN: 9798671584479

To all the parents and teachers —
We've always been superheroes - this year we just get a
cool new costume to help our superpowers come to life.
— E.O.

Everyone knows that the end of last school year was wild, but this year we will start things with a new and unique style. The time has come, and we're finally back at school - Yay! We know that this whole idea is crazy, and some people may even say it's outrageous. However, life must go on regardless of whether or not a virus is contagious. This year, we've taken some measures to help us get off to a safe start, even if it does have to be from 6 feet apart.

Masks

Masks are the first thing you'll notice that may seem a bit weird, but your friend is not wearing a mask to hide his cool new beard. It's important that you wear your mask over your mouth and your nose, this is the only place that it goes. The mask should be worn while walking through the hallway, and even while sitting in your seat. Don't be silly, the mask is not to be worn on your feet. When not wearing your mask, keep it someplace specific, your teacher will likely give you a mask storage idea that's terrific!

Gloves

Some people may be wearing gloves, and that's okay too. The purpose is to help them stay safe, while they do their job and help you. When you wear gloves, you may think that you're a mime. It's okay to practice those miming skills - you just can't do it all the time. For some people opening doors with a glove may become the new norm. We can think of gloves as part of a new superhero uniform.

Hand Washing

Everyone will wash their hands often throughout the day, because we know that our hands are a place where germs like to stay. If we cough or sneeze we'll do it into our elbow pocket. That's one of the easiest ways for germs to travel, so like ninjas we'll block it!

Hand Sanitizer

Hand sanitizer stations are set-up everywhere, you just wait and see. Using them frequently to stay healthy will definitely be key. If you're outside playing and you can't get to a sink and some actual soap, please use the sanitizer before touching any equipment, even a jump rope. When using sanitizer you must rub until dry, because no one wants to be that drippy hand guy.

Supplies

Normally your teacher begs you to share your supplies, but right now things are different, let's remember that guys! This year, there are some things you just shouldn't share, and we'll label those things and treat them with care. So make sure to follow the new procedures that have been put in place, and keep all of your stuff in your personal space.

Social distancing

One of the biggest changes will be to try to stay 6 feet apart. We know it will be hard, especially at the start, but think of these tips and try to do your part. Here are some things that 6 feet may look like - for example, the length of an awesome double seater bike. The size of a tub is also an excellent way to measure or even three pirate's chests lined up and filled with treasure. A dolphin can also be six feet in length or a bodybuilder holding up a car and showing his strength. Just think of the 6 foot rule as creating your own personal bubble, a perfect way to keep you healthy and not get in to trouble.

We know it may feel strange to be here, but you have nothing to fear. Your parents, teachers, and anyone else who takes care of you, are all educated on exactly what to do. Don't worry, this year we will still have loads of fun, but your safety will always be priority number one. Whether it's September, October, November, or December, this will undoubtedly be a school year that you will always remember. So try your best to just listen and do your part, then this unique back-to-school thing will be a breeze from the start.

ABOUT THE AUTHOR

Emily was born and raised in upstate New York. She currently lives in Tampa, Florida with her husband and two daughters. She's an elementary teacher who has always had a love for writing. Emily was losing sleep each night worrying about how she was going to explain what school will look like to her daughter when she begins Pre-K during a pandemic. She needed a way to explain the unique protocols that her students, and own children, would encounter in an age-appropriate way. Emily hopes that other parents and teachers find this book to be a helpful tool when transitioning their kiddos back to school during a pandemic.

Big Guava Books

ADDITIONAL INFORMATION & RESOURCES

Check out BigGuavaBooks.com or follow @bigguavabooks on Instagram for follow-up activities that can be used with this book. Activities include modeling with clay, worksheets, ideas for foldables, anchor charts, a classroom bulletin board display, and much more!

Made in the USA
Monee, IL
14 April 2021